My 1st Classic Story

The DONKEY in the LION'S SKIN

A retelling of Aesop's Fable
by Eric Blair

illustrated by Dianne Silverman

PICTURE WINDOW BOOKS
a capstone imprint

My First Classic Story is published by Picture Window Books
A Capstone Imprint
151 Good Counsel Drive, P.O. Box 669
Mankato, Minnesota 56002
www.capstonepub.com

Library of Congress Cataloging-in-Publication Data
Blair, Eric.
The donkey in the lion's skin: a retelling of Aesop's fable / retold by
Eric Blair; illustrated by Dianne Silverman.
p. cm. — (My first classic story)
Summary: After putting on a lion disguise, a silly donkey amuses
himself by frightening all of the animals in the forest until he meets a
clever fox.
ISBN 978-1-4048-6506-8 (library binding)
[1. Fables. 2. Folklore.] I. Silverman, Dianne, ill. II. Aesop. III. Title.
IV. Series.
PZ8.2.B595Do 2011
398.2—dc22
[E]   2010050975

Art Director: Kay Fraser
Graphic Designer: Emily Harris
Production Specialist: Sarah Bennett

Printed in the United States of America in Stevens Point, Wisconsin.
032011
006111WZF11

What Is a Fable?

A fable is a story that teaches a lesson. In some fables, animals may talk and act the way people do. A Greek slave named Aesop created some of the world's favorite fables. Aesop's fables have been enjoyed for more than 2,000 years.

Once there was a foolish donkey.

One day, he found the skin of a lion. "I can pretend to be a lion with this," thought the donkey.

"It will be fun to scare the other animals,"
he said with a laugh.

The donkey put on the skin. It made him feel brave.

The silly donkey roamed around the country in disguise. He growled, "Grrr! Grrr!"

When animals and people saw the donkey, they were scared. They thought the donkey was a lion. They ran away.

The donkey watched the animals run
away from him.

He was proud of himself. He let out a loud bray.

A clever fox heard the bray. The donkey did not fool him.

He knew the donkey was just playing a trick.

18

"You are a fool! Take off that silly costume," the fox said.

19

20

"You look like a lion. But by the way you bray, you can only be a donkey," said the fox.

21

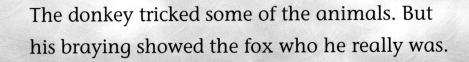

The donkey tricked some of the animals. But his braying showed the fox who he really was.

You can pretend to be something you are not. But in the end, the truth will come out.

The End